King
Emmett
the
Second

MARY STOLZ

King
Emmett
the
Second

pictures by Garth Williams

A Yearling Book

Published by
Dell Publishing
a division of
Bantam Doubleday Dell Publishing Group, Inc.
666 Fifth Avenue
New York, New York 10103

The trademark Yearling® is registered in the U.S. Patent and Trademark Office.

The trademark Dell® is registered in the U.S. Patent and Trademark Office.

ISBN: 0-440-40777-X

Reprinted by arrangement with William Morrow & Company, Inc., on behalf of Greenwillow Books

Printed in the United States of America

April 1993

10 9 8 7 6 5 4 3 2

WES

For Susan again,
and with fond recall,
for Paul

Contents

CHAPTER ONE

7

CHAPTER TWO

17

CHAPTER THREE

30

CHAPTER FOUR

40

CHAPTER FIVE

49

CHAPTER ONE

"Good news!" said Mr. Murphy at breakfast one May morning.

Emmett looked up happily. "We're going to the farm to see King Emmett? At *last*?" he added.

Mr. Murphy looked at Mrs. Murphy. They sighed.

"No, Emmett. The good news is that I got the job I

was hoping for, and we are going to move away from this noisy, dirty city to a nice small town in Ohio."

Emmett's mouth opened, closed, opened again. "That's not good news! That's awful news! I don't want to move to Ohio! I won't move to Ohio!"

"We can't afford to buy a house out there and keep up this apartment for you," said his mother.

"Then what are we going to *do*?"

"Only one answer to that. You come with us."

Emmett bit his lip, looked from his mother to his father, thought for a moment, then threw himself on the floor. He screamed and hollered and rolled around.

It was the first temper tantrum he had ever had, and he made it a good one.

When he got tired, he sat up and glared. "I won't go!"

"Oh yes," said his father. "You will." He looked a little annoyed, a little sad, and very firm. "We are moving at the end of the month."

Emmett realized that they were going to win. He held

his breath for a while, but his parents continued eating their toast and coffee and paid no attention to him.

He got up and went to his room, where he sat on the floor and thought for a while about how he was going to hate Ohio.

He looked around him.

There they all were—his pigs.

Bank pigs, paper pigs, wooden pigs, glass pigs.

On the table was a half-finished pig jigsaw puzzle.

On the bed was his pink stuffed pig with yellow button eyes.

On the table beside the bed was a pig-shaped lamp.

On the bookshelves were books about pigs.

On the walls were pictures of pigs. Some he had cut out of magazines; some he had drawn himself. One was a calendar three years old.

One—the best of all—was a poster of Emmett standing in the snow beside a fine great pig.

Mr. Murphy had taken the picture one time when they were snowed in at the farm, and had it made into a poster.

King Emmett and Emmett were standing together outside King Emmett's private sty, and in the way of pictures and posters, there they would always be.

King Emmett was Emmett's very own live pig, though he lived on a farm upstate. He was a present for Emmett's last birthday.

Emmett kept in touch with his pig. He wrote letters to Mr. and Mrs. Carson, who owned the farm where King Emmett was a boarder, and he sent them some of his allowance for treats like baloney, a special favorite of King Emmett's.

King Emmett's way of keeping in touch was to wait.

Every month the Murphys drove upstate to the farm so that Emmett could spend the day with his pet.

Emmett and King Emmett would walk up a hill at the back of the farm to a place they'd found that was nice and private. They would play a game they'd thought up. King Emmett was very smart. He could retrieve a ball. Emmett would throw it; King Emmett would bring it back to him.

When they got tired of playing, Emmett would get out a small baloney roll and watch lovingly as King Emmett gulped it down.

Then they'd sit together on the grass. Sometimes Emmett would talk, and King Emmett always paid close attention.

But they hadn't been to the farm for a long time. Whenever Emmett asked why not, his parents changed the subject.

Emmett got up and went to the living room, where his mother was watering plants. It was past nine o'clock, and his father had left for the office, where he still worked. Until the end of the month, Emmett supposed.

"I'm sorry I had the temper tantrum," he said loudly.

Mrs. Murphy turned and said, "Well. I guess it's understandable. I hope you don't make a habit of it."

Emmett didn't say he would and didn't say he wouldn't.

He said, "We haven't been to the farm in a long time."

"I know, dear."

"I want to go and see King Emmett."

"I know, dear."

"But that's not an *answer.*"

"You didn't ask a question. You just said something." She looked at the ceiling, at the floor, at the telephone, and out of a window.

When she ran out of places to look, she turned to Emmett and said, "You're right, of course."

"*Why* haven't we been to the farm?" Emmett said, and added, "That's a question."

"Oh, yes. It certainly is." But she didn't answer it.

"Anyway, I can write him a letter," Emmett said. "I want to tell him about the new zoo. And I'll send him ten cents for baloney."

His mother looked at him for a long time before she said, "Emmett, there is something I have to tell you."

Emmett had learned that when there was something his parents had to tell him, it was *never* something he wanted to hear.

"I think I'll go for a walk," he told her.

"No, dear. You have to hear this, and I guess—" She stopped and sighed. His parents did seem to sigh a lot. "I guess since your father is so busy getting ready for his new job, it's up to me to tell you."

"I think I'll go make my bed."

But his mother pulled him down on the sofa beside her, put her arm around him, and said, "Dear Emmett. Listen to me. King Emmett is dead."

Emmett twisted around and stared at her. He couldn't speak. He didn't cry. He just stared without blinking.

"My love, you must know that everything that lives must someday die."

Emmett shook his head violently. "Not me. Or you or Daddy."

"Well—we won't and you won't for years and years and years."

That seemed long enough.

But Emmett found that he was going to cry, and he didn't want to. He didn't know what he wanted. For her not to have told him this. For King Emmett not to be dead. He thought maybe he wanted to go to sleep.

"Why did he die?" he said. "Why did that happen? He looked big and beautiful and—last time we went to see—last time he was—"

He stopped, because he couldn't go on.

"Well, you see . . . the fact is, and surely, surely you must know this, Emmett, when a piglet grows up, he becomes a boar."

"No!" Emmett shouted. "King Emmett is never a bore!"

"Oh my. The word I'm using is spelled differently."

"I don't care how—"

His mother interrupted. "A b-o-r-e, Emmett, is . . ." She thought a moment. "An example of a b-o-r-e is someone who has temper tantrums. Yes, that's a good example. But a b-o-a-r is a pig who has grown up, who is no longer a piglet, and can no longer be a little boy's pet."

"Why should that make him die?"

"Emmett! Pigs are bred and brought *up* to provide food for people. That's their purpose."

"Not for me, it isn't!" Emmett shouted. "That's horrible, horrible, horrible!"

He ran to his room. He slammed the door and sat on the floor and pushed his fists against his face.

All he wanted was for King Emmett still to be there on the farm, waiting for Emmett to come to him, waiting to walk to the place at the top of the hill and play their game and then sit quietly, just being together.

He thought of different times.

He thought how King Emmett would always grunt a greeting when he saw Emmett coming.

He remembered the night when he and his parents had been snowed in on the farm, and how he'd gone to sleep, snug under the puffy quilt, thinking about King Emmett, snug, too—out of the storm, in his clean sty on his shining straw.

It had made him feel happy, thinking how one of them was warm in his bed in the house and the other was warm in his sty in the straw, while the snow fell in the night.

And now?

If the snow fell, or the rain did, or the moon came out or did not, King Emmett would never sleep in his clean sty on the farm again.

And now?

Now King Emmett was gone.

He was nowhere.

King Emmett, his pig, his friend that he loved . . . was dead.

Emmett put his head on his knees and stayed very still for a long time.

CHAPTER TWO

M r. and Mrs. Murphy and Emmett stood on one side of a wide-board fence, looking at a house on the other side.

It was the sort of house they made Christmas cards about, except now there wasn't any snow. A wooden house, with a porch going across the front and halfway around the side. Emmett could see that it had an attic, because of the small windows on the third floor.

The only attic he had ever been in was at Mr. and Mrs. Carson's farm. It was a good place to go and be mad in—sort of cobwebby and gloomy. Now he had an attic of his very own to be mad in, instead of just going to his room and slamming the door.

His mother said he should say "angry, not mad," but either way he got that way pretty often. He didn't know why. His parents were nice to him about it, which made him even madder. Or maybe angrier.

He didn't know why about that, either.

"Well, Emmett? What do you think?"

That was his father—asking what did he think.

"Do you like it?"

That was his mother—asking if he liked it.

Emmett didn't answer.

Instead, he stared at the place where they were going to live from now on. He had grown up in New York City, and this was the second real house he would ever be in.

The other was the farm where Mr. and Mrs. Carson lived.

Where King Emmett had lived, in days that seemed long and longer ago.

Emmett had found that he could not think about King Emmett every minute.

He had found, as the weeks passed, that being sad was not something he could do all the time, every day.

There were times when just *thinking* about King Emmett made him burst into pain.

But there were other times when he didn't think about him at all.

Now, far from the hilltop where he and his pig had been together, he stood with his parents and stared at this house while they waited for him to say something about it.

He had told them and *told* them that he was going to hate Ohio and everything in Ohio.

It was his duty to hate Ohio, and this town, and this house, because it was all too far away from home. *His* home was an apartment across the street from the Central Park Zoo, which he could go to whenever he liked, if somebody went with him.

This house was a place he had to live in from now on, thousands of miles from where he and King Emmett . . .

He tried to stop thinking backward.

Think about now. About here.

Living in this house, he would never see Mr. and Mrs. Carson again, or the elevator man that he liked, or his dentist that he liked, too. Or Pepper, the Airedale from the fifth floor. He wouldn't get to go to the zoo again. Probably he'd never see his friend Jimmy Bredon again.

He was going to go to school in Ohio and get there on a school bus, with a lot of *strangers.*

Standing now on one side of the fence, looking at the house, his parents were asking what did he think and did he like it, and it was time for him to answer.

His mind was made up.

"I hate it," he said.

"Well!" Mr. Murphy spoke in a pretending-to-be-jolly voice. "Can't stand out here till nightfall. Shall we see what Emmett hates about the inside, now that he's decided about the outside?"

Emmett scowled.

He did not care for it when his father talked that way—as if everything Emmett said were sort of funny.

He tried to think of good reasons to give them, leaving out King Emmett, because he knew what had happened to his pig was not their fault.

"There isn't a zoo to go to anymore," he said.

"Of course there is. A fine zoo, in Cincinnati."

Emmett hadn't known that.

"It's not right across the street," he pointed out.

"No," said his mother. "We couldn't arrange that."

"I have to start school on a *bus* with a lot of *strangers*, instead of with Jimmy. I hate that."

"Not for three months yet," said Mrs. Murphy. "Maybe you'll change your mind by then."

"I won't. I don't want to ride on a bus. I don't want to live in a house. I want to live in an apartment."

"Well, you aren't going to," said his father. He sounded sort of snappy.

"There's a garden out back," said Mrs. Murphy. She sounded sort of tired. "You can grow vegetables, just like Mrs. Carson."

"I hate vegetables."

"No, you don't. You like asparagus."

"Not anymore."

There was a long silence.

Then Mr. Murphy said, "I repeat. We probably should go inside. Get the inspection over. You *hear* me, Emmett?"

"Yes, Daddy."

"Then get cracking."

□   □   □

In the room that was to be Emmett's, he found that his pig collection—paper, glass, bank, stuffed, calendar, jigsaw, books, lamp—was in place.

The poster of him and King Emmett was on a wall by itself.

Emmett swallowed hard before he managed to say, "I don't like it."

"Grand," said Mr. Murphy. "Dandy."

Emmett wondered whether to have a temper tantrum. "I *told* you—" he began angrily, but his mother interrupted.

"We heard. Let's go back out and walk around. We have two whole acres here, Emmett. Lots of room to play in."

"There's no one to play with."

"Oh, I expect there'll be someone pretty soon. There are neighbors with children."

"I don't know them. And I don't—"

"We'll *all* make friends here. Wait and see."

"I don't *want* any friends."

He wondered what Jimmy was doing right this minute, back in New York City.

Back home, where everybody belonged.

"Nobody's forcing you," said Mr. Murphy.

Outside, there was plenty of room for a garden. There were lots of big trees. One tree had a rope and wood swing dangling from a thick branch.

"The people who lived here before us left it for you," his mother explained.

"How could they leave it for me? They don't know me."

"They left it for the boy I said we had living with us. Our son, Emmett, I told them, who hates Ohio without seeing it."

"Well. Well, that was nice of them," said Emmett.

He did try to be fair, when he thought about it.

He ran to the swing, hopped on, swung out as far as he could, and fell off when he got to the top.

Now he could really let loose.

He screamed and yelled and doubled up, choking.

His father picked him up. His mother looked at the scrape on the knee that he had fallen on.

"That's not so bad," she said.

Emmett screamed louder.

"Hospital, do you think?" asked Mr. Murphy. "Or can we take care of this ourselves?"

"We'll manage. You carry him in, and I'll get the first-aid kit."

"I wouldn't cry," Emmett said, still crying, as they sprayed his knee with something and then put a Band-Aid on it, "if it was the *other* knee. It's just that—" He gulped and sobbed.

"Just that what?" his father asked.

Emmett touched the Band-Aid and winced. "This is my favorite knee," he explained. "I don't care what happens to the other one."

"You like one of your knees better than the other one?"

"I always have."

"I see. You never told us."

Emmett sniffled.

The day passed, and they had dinner. Then they went out on the front porch and sat on some wicker chairs, which the same people had probably left behind. Anyway, Emmett had never seen them before.

One chair was a rocker, and Emmett got to it first.

They were tired. The only sound was the rumble of the rocker going back and forth on the wooden floor.

A boy went past on a bicycle, riding lazily, hands clasped behind his head. Emmett stiffened.

An enemy already, maybe!

You never could tell with strangers.

The boy saw them and suddenly leaned forward, grasped the handlebars, and jerked his bike onto its back wheel, making it rear. Like a horse. He dropped to two wheels again, sailed into a driveway across the street, propped the bike against a tree, and went into the house there.

"He looks pleasant," said Mrs. Murphy.

"Sure can handle a bike," said Mr. Murphy.

"Thinks he's so great, riding a two-wheeler," said Emmett. He could do that, too. If he wanted to. If he had a bike.

He and Jimmy didn't have bikes because their parents said they wouldn't be safe, riding on the sidewalks of New York City.

"Bet he thinks he's hot stuff," Emmett said.

"Oh dear," said his mother, and sighed.

"Would you like to have a bike?" Mr. Murphy asked.

"No."

Now his father sighed.

"You do that an awful lot," Emmett pointed out.

"Do what?" his mother asked.

"Breathe *out* like that," he said crossly.

"Goodness," said Mr. Murphy. "Why in the world would we do that?"

Emmett pretended not to hear.

There were countryish sounds. Almost, Emmett thought, like the sounds at the farm.

Not quite.

No cows lowing from the meadow.

No rooster stepping about the place stiff-legged, stopping now and then to cock-a-doodle-doo. No hens cackling from their house.

No sounds of *pigs*.

Piglets made marvelous mixed-up squealings, falling over each other to get to their mother's milk.

Big pigs grunted and snorted and made sounds like *oink.*

King Emmett had always oinked a greeting from his sty when he heard Emmett coming.

No more, no more. King Emmett was gone.

Emmett blinked and looked at his hands, keeping very, very still until he was sure he wouldn't cry.

Just the same, it was kind of countryish here.

Birds, invisible in the trees, singing.

Grasshoppers or crickets twiddling in the grass.

Greenish lights of fireflies flicking on here, off there—all over the dark that was coming on.

A bat whirled around a streetlamp out on the road.

"I guess it's not so bad here," he said. "In a way."

His father smiled, and his mother said, "That's good, dear. We're happy to hear it."

And so to bed.

CHAPTER THREE

A couple of weeks later Emmett said to himself that if it wasn't so bad here, it wasn't so good either.

He still hadn't made any friends.

The enemy across the street was always prancing on his bike—riding with his hands behind his head, spinning on the back wheel, lifting the front wheel off the ground, leaning from one side to the other till you thought he'd fall off but he never did.

They hadn't spoken to each other.

There were other kids, of course.

He hadn't spoken to any of them either.

He sure did miss Jimmy Bredon.

He missed the elevator man, and the lady on the fifth floor and Pepper, her Airedale, and the man who sold ice-cream cones over in Central Park, and the lion keeper at the zoo and—

More than any of them, he missed his friend King Emmett.

His mother bought him a bicycle.

When his father came home from work that evening, Emmett ran toward him down the driveway.

"She got me a two-wheeler!" he yelled furiously.

Mr. Murphy got out of his car, locked it, put the keys in his pocket.

"Who's *she*?" he asked. "The cat's mother?"

Emmett stuck his lower lip out and narrowed his eyes. "She's *my* mother. You know that."

"So why do you call her *she?*"

"All *right*. My *mother.*"

"Lacks proper feeling, but we'll let it pass. Now, what's the problem?"

"She bought me a two-wheeler!"

"We decided you ought to have one. Or anyway, would like to have one. Not, of course, if it makes you angry."

"It's got training wheels!"

"Ah. Oh. I see." Mr. Murphy cleared his throat. "Let's go in, shall we? Look the situation over."

"I won't ride a bike with training wheels!"

In the kitchen, Mrs. Murphy was putting her special lasagne in the oven, but she turned and pointed toward the back porch. "It's out there. I guess I made a mistake."

"It's dopey and dumb, and I won't *ride* a bike with training wheels. I don't *want* a bike with—"

"Shut up," said Mr. Murphy.

That was a surprise. Mr. Murphy didn't usually tell people to shut up.

Emmett stopped talking but dragged his father by the hand to the back porch and pointed.

There was a small red two-wheeler. It was, sure enough, equipped with a pair of training wheels.

"Good-looking bike," said Mr. Murphy.

"I thought so," said Mrs. Murphy. "And about the— the you-know-whats . . . well, he's never been on a bike." She turned to Emmett. "You've never ridden a bike before. I thought you'd need trai—those things— just to start with . . ."

"I won't ride a bike that has—"

"Say that once more, Emmett," Mr. Murphy said, "and you won't ride a bike till you're thirty years old."

"Well, I just bet you I do—" Emmett began, then found his father smiling at him.

"It's really very simple, Emmett. Not worth all this fuss. We remove the training wheels. See?"

"Yes, but she—Mother—she thinks I *need* them."

Mr. Murphy looked at his wife. "Do you still think so?" he asked.

"My goodness, *no!*"

"Will you take off the—those things—*now?*" Emmett demanded. "So I can go out and ride my bike?"

"I'll take them off, but you can't ride it, or I should say *practice* riding it, until tomor—"

"Why *not?*" Emmett shouted. "It's still light out!"

"Because."

"That's not an answer."

"You sometimes think it is."

"Anyway," said Mrs. Murphy, "we're practically ready for dinner."

"I'm not ready."

"Oh, yes, you are."

"But I want to ride my—"

"Emmett!" His father was almost yelling.

Emmett decided it would be better if he waited until tomorrow to ride his bike.

Practice riding it.

He bet he'd be pretty good at it.

In the morning, having promised to stay on the sidewalk, he took his bike down the drive and out the front gate.

There he carefully positioned it to be upright. Holding on to the fence, he got aboard, steadied himself, and shoved off.

Wobbling a few feet, he fell off to the right, hitting the sidewalk, falling on the knee that didn't matter.

But it hurt. It hurt a lot. Emmett was a boy who thought he had a right to cry when something hurt.

Not now.

The enemy across the street was sitting on his front steps.

Looking at Emmett.

Watching.

Thinks he's hot stuff, Emmett growled to himself. Just because he got a head start on bike riding.

I'll show him.

Setting his jaw, he climbed back on the two-wheeler, zigzagged a yard or two, fell to the left, landing on his favorite knee.

That *really* hurt.

For a second he stayed where he was, on all fours, on the sidewalk, not making a sound.

When he looked up, the across-the-street boy was coming toward him, walking slowly.

Emmett, slowly, too, got to his feet, swallowing hard.

This fellow was pretty big. At least a couple of years older than Emmett, and probably—well, who knew what he weighed, but it looked like plenty.

Emmett was pretty skinny.

He stuck out his lower lip, narrowed his eyes, clenched his fists, and waited.

"Want me to steady you for a few times?" said the enemy.

"Huh?"

"That's how my brother taught me. He held the back

of the saddle and ran behind me. Till I got the balance, you know."

"Oh?" Emmett was dumbfounded, and still wary. "Did he? I mean, did you?"

"Yup. It worked fine."

"Oh. I see."

Not an enemy after all? After all, a sort of nice kid, offering to help?

"How long did it take you? To balance on it?"

"Not long. An hour, maybe. Want to give it a try?"

They did, and in about an hour Emmett was riding up and down without falling off.

He'd get to hands behind his head and spinning on one wheel and that sort of thing after a bit. For now, to be able to ride down the block, stay in the saddle, wheel, and come whizzing back, all without falling off was enough to make him very pleased with himself.

And pleased with Cruz Ramirez, the boy from across the street.

Emmett had never known a person named Cruz before. He thought it was a neat name.

He thought Cruz was pretty neat all around.

He asked his mother if Cruz could have lunch with them, and she said of course.

After that they went out and sat on the porch. Emmett let Cruz have the rocker.

They talked.

Cruz told Emmett he'd ride with him on the school bus when the time came. That was a big relief.

"How do you like it here?" Cruz asked.

"I don't," Emmett said promptly.

"Why not?"

"It's too far from home."

"Isn't this your home?"

"Well. I live here."

"Isn't that the same thing?"

Emmett frowned. "I suppose so," he admitted.

He looked at the lawn, and the big trees, and the quiet road, and the houses. "It's all right, I guess. Maybe pretty nice."

"Sure it is. Where did you live before?"

"In New York City."

"Wow. I've never been to New York City. Been to Cincinnati a lot, of course."

"I haven't been there yet. My mother says there's a good zoo there."

"Oh, sure. And we've got a great ball team. The Reds."

Emmett didn't know much about ball teams. But he could learn. If he wanted to.

Meanwhile—he'd learned to ride his bike. Without training wheels.

That was what was important.

He and Cruz became friends.

CHAPTER FOUR

E mmett was lying in bed, hands behind his head, thinking.

Things that he thought he thought often turned out to be different from what he'd thought he'd thought to begin with.

Things that he said would happen for *sure* would turn out to be not for sure at all.

He had said he was going to hate living in Ohio instead of in New York City.

He didn't hate it.

He had told his parents he would hate living in a house instead of in an apartment.

He liked living here.

He liked his room; he liked the kitchen, the yard, the swing, the garden. He liked the attic, where he and Cruz played caveman on rainy days.

In fact, he liked the whole house.

He had told them and *told* them he would never make any friends if they moved to Ohio.

He had made friends all up and down the road.

One day his mother said, "How pleasant—that you don't go around anymore saying how many things you hate. That was tiresome."

"It sure tired me," said Emmett.

"And you haven't had a temper tantrum in *ages.*"

"No."

"Maybe you'll never have one again."

Emmett didn't say he would and didn't say he wouldn't.

Tonight, after his mother had finished the sixth chapter of *Stuart Little*, brave mouse, because Emmett didn't want to hear pig stories anymore, she closed the book, put it aside, and *looked* at him.

"Why are you looking at me?" he asked grumpily.

"Well," said his mother, "we've been thinking—"

Emmett waited.

"Your birthday is next week," said Mrs. Murphy.

"I know that."

"Well," Mrs. Murphy said again. "It's like this. We've been wondering. . . ."

Emmett waited some more.

"What we wonder," his mother said in a rush, "is— would you like to have another pig?"

When Emmett folded in his lips and didn't speak, she said, "Look—there's a small farm we've found where the farmer would be willing—"

She stopped because Emmett seemed not to hear. He was staring at the poster on the wall.

There they were, he and his pig, in the snow, in front of the sty. Emmett was smiling. King Emmett seemed to be smiling, too.

Oh, it had been such a wonderful day! And there it would always be—that perfect day.

He said, "Would the same thing happen to him that happened to King Emmett?"

"Well, dear, you have to understand—"

"That means it would."

His mother sighed.

"I don't *want* a pig. I don't want any pet at all."

"Most children want one, even if it's not a pig," said Mrs. Murphy.

"I don't. I don't *ever* want one."

So she kissed him good night and went downstairs.

Emmett lay for a long time with his hands behind his head.

Thinking.

Outside, a whippoorwill trilled on and on. He hadn't heard a whippoorwill until they moved here. He wouldn't have minded never hearing one at all.

Owl sounds were good—lonely and hooty and soft in the night. A saw-whet that lived in a tree behind the house whistled *too tooo toooo too.* . . .

His mother and father were right. They always were. Almost always. Sometimes that annoyed him, and sometimes it made him feel safe.

He *had* been noticing pets.

Other people's pets.

He'd been thinking—thinking—

He'd been thinking that *maybe*, someday, he *might* just—just *think* about—

Again he looked at the poster, to find King Emmett smiling at him.

Did the smile say he knew that he would always be first, a pig and a pet like no other pig or pet in the world?

That he knew he would never be forgotten?

Emmett thought he could see all that in King Emmett's smile.

Most people had pets of some kind. There were the usual ones on this road, and some pretty funny ones.

He thought now about all those different creatures. Mostly dogs or cats, of course. But birds, too, and mice, fish, gerbils, even a box turtle. . . .

Cruz Ramirez had an orange cockatoo that climbed about on the branches of a tree trunk on the Ramirezes' enclosed back porch.

Tangerine, her name was. She was the color of orange sherbet, and was a talking bird.

She could almost say her name.

She could say, "*Oh* dear!" and *"Donde está Cruz?"* and "Lemonade, amigo?"

After Cruz told you what she was saying, you knew it wasn't something else.

Emmett thought she was beautiful, and sort of interesting, but not very.

Four houses down lived the Parker twins. They were named Patrick and Petunia.

"Alas!" Mrs. Murphy said when she heard that.

But the twins were very nice and had a pool that they invited everybody into.

They had a little yippy, nippy dog that Mr. Murphy said looked like a fur-bearing grasshopper.

Chip Martin, who lived next door to the Murphys on one side, had a pet box turtle, Friday, that lived in a weedy patch in their yard.

Friday would come when you called him. Her. Sometimes.

Friday lived on grasses and crickets and berries. Chip put slices of banana near the weedy patch every morning, and every evening they were gone.

Now and then the turtle would come lifting out of the weeds on clawed webby feet, turning a celery-shaped head from side to side, looking about through heavy lids.

Emmett thought Friday was a fine turtle but didn't want one of his own.

Chrissy Drigo, who lived in the other direction from Cruz, had a big fancy aquarium. Emmett quite enjoyed watching all the small bright fish go darting among fronds of seaweed. An aerator sent up a stream of clear, babbling bubbles.

A nice thing to own, that aquarium.

Emmett didn't want one.

The McCrays, a very old couple who lived across the street, had a very old marmalade cat, Fanshawe.

Emmett liked cats. They always seemed to know what they wanted and how to get it. He admired that. But his father was allergic to them, so cats were out of the question.

A boy far down the road, Chas Broder, kept white mice in a cage. They had a wheel for running in, and it made Emmett sad to watch them racing and racing, trying to get somewhere.

The Mahoney boys had gerbils.

Emmett didn't want a pet that got kept in a cage.

With a start that made him sit up, he realized he was trying to decide what sort of pet he *did* want.

Was this forgetting King Emmett?

NO!

Never in his life would he forget King Emmett.

Flopping back down, he pulled the pillow over his head and told himself to go to sleep.

CHAPTER FIVE

The world hung hot and still, melting in the sun. Emmett and his parents were on the porch, talking. About dogs.

"When I was a girl," Mrs. Murphy said, "I had a puppy named Scrappy. What a scrappy little scrap of a thing he was."

"What kind?" Emmett asked.

"Oh, no *kind*. Just a dog."

"The Petersons have this chocolate brown Labrador. It's a thoroughbred," said Emmett.

"Those are good dogs," said Mr. Murphy. "Labradors. But a dog doesn't have to be a thoroughbred to be a good dog."

"I know that," said Emmett.

"I had three dogs when I was growing up," said his father. "Not all at once. One after the other."

"Did they *die?*" Emmett asked.

"Well—yes. But they had long lives, happy lives, I think."

"You mean when one would die, then you'd go get another one? Just like that?"

"Emmett! Not just like *that*. Not right away. I never *replaced* one. Each dog was very special. But—" He shrugged. "I loved dogs, so after a while, yes—my parents would get me another one."

"That didn't mean you forgot the ones before."

"Of course not."

"Why didn't we have a dog when we lived in New York City? I mean, if you and Mom are so fond of them?"

"New York City didn't seem to us the place to bring up a dog."

"But this is," Emmett said thoughtfully.

For a long time they remained silent. Emmett rocked. Mr. Murphy knocked his heels on the wooden floor. Mrs. Murphy waved to Cruz and his parents as they got in their car to go someplace.

"Could I—could we—I think I would like to have a dog," Emmett said breathlessly. "For my birthday."

There.

He had told them. He had said the words.

"That's a *good* idea." His parents spoke at the same time.

Another silence. Then Mr. Murphy said, "Do you

have an idea of what sort of—"

"No."

"What I think—" said Mrs. Murphy, and stopped.

They turned to her.

"I think we should go to the animal shelter. There is always some dog—or cat—waiting in a shelter for somebody to come and say, '*There* you are! I've been looking for you!'" She smiled at her son. "There's nothing wrong with buying a dog, Emmett. A thoroughbred. But when I remember Scrappy—waiting in the pound, as if he were waiting just for me to come and find him—"

Emmett's heart began to thump. "Could we go now? Could we?"

"Of course," said his father.

Driving the three or so miles to the animal shelter, Emmett found that he was very nervous. Suppose there wasn't a dog waiting for him to come and say, "*There* you are! I've been looking for you!"

Suppose the dogs in the shelter just looked at him and looked away?

Suppose there weren't any dogs there at all?

He knew all at once that he couldn't bear it if he didn't find the dog that was waiting just for him.

Didn't find him *today*.

"Maybe there won't be any dogs?" he whispered.

"There are always dogs. Waiting there. Always," Mr. Murphy said.

"And cats," said Mrs. Murphy. She was awfully fond of cats, but she wasn't complaining. If a person was allergic to cats, you didn't get a cat.

Parking at the shelter, they heard sounds that made it plain that many dogs were waiting.

Emmett, while his father and mother talked to a woman at the desk, shifted from foot to foot.

His mouth was dry. It was hard for him to breathe. Soon he would know.

"As it happens," the woman was saying, "a man just brought his dog to be left here. He was crying. The man was. I mean, we could tell that it was breaking his heart, leaving King—"

"King?" said the Murphys, all together.

"Why, yes. That's the dog's name. He's a mixture of dogs. A lovely boy, not even a year old."

"Then why did the owner—"

"He couldn't tell us. He was too unhappy. He just said please, please be sure that King finds someone who will love him."

"Oh, I will, I *will*," cried Emmett.

"But, son, you haven't seen him yet."

"I don't have to. I want him. I'll love him."

The woman looked at Mr. and Mrs. Murphy.

Emmett's father said, "It's the name. King. Our son had a—had a pet he loved very much. His name was King Emmett."

"Well. Well, isn't that a coincidence. All right, then. I'll just go back and fetch him out here, and we'll see, shall we?"

King came into the room looking around for someone he needed to see but didn't find. He stopped and eyed Emmett, who made no move.

In a moment, cautiously, still turning his head from side to side, he moved toward Emmett, who put his hand out.

King leaned forward, touched a finger with his nose, looked up.

Their eyes met.

King sat. He put a paw up to be taken.

Emmett took it.

Then he took the dog's head in his arms.

"Well," said the woman. "I guess that will do, all right. Now, if you will just sign these papers, and there's the matter of a small fee. . . ."

In the car King lay across Emmett's lap in the back seat.

Whether the dog was remembering the man who had cried and left him at the shelter, or the boy was thinking of a pig called King Emmett, who knew?

They were together. The boy and the dog.

When he could speak, Emmett said, "I'm going to name him King Emmett the Second, after King Emmett the First. But we'll call him King."

King waved his tail quietly as they drove toward their home in Ohio.